GUTSY

Hi JACKIE & DON
HOPE You ENJOY THE BOOK
DAVID.   XMAS. 2010

Published by
Attree Publishing
243, Canterbury Road,
Margate, Kent
CT9 5JR
David Attree has asserted his
right under the copyright,
design and patent act 1988 to
be identified as the author of
this work.

Original Manuscript written by
David Attree.

DAVID ATTREE

GUTSY
The Golf Ball

PREFACE

I thought it would make a nice change for you humans to know what it's like to be a golf ball. Describing how we feel, what we see and what we hear, which I am afraid is a lot of swearing.

In this light-hearted look at playing golf through my eyes, I have tried to make it more challenging by arranging the book so that each hole is a typical eighteen holes of golf played by a high handicap golfer.

Humans, be prepared to be embarrassed.

1st HOLE

Par 4

Hi, my name is Gutsy the golf ball, I am due to start my round on the assault course.

Humans call this place a golf course.

That's a joke, the places some of them get into, I am sure it's as much an assault course to them as it is to me.

Unfortunately, anything can happen to me out there on the course, the reason being, the players that get to play with me aren't exactly good, if you get my drift.

Today I have a guy called Richard. I will have great pleasure in calling him, Dick.

Anyway, it looks like Dick is ready to tee off, heaven help me.

Here I am sitting on the tee peg looking down the fairway, I will be very surprised if that is where I end up.

Dick is looking at me nervously because it's the first tee. This is quite normal for humans.

Mind you, I'm nervous too, sitting here waiting to have my ass kicked.

Here comes the club head, ouch! That hurt more than it should, must be a slice.

I am going straight for the trees on the right. Phew! Just missed that big tree and landed softly in some long damp grass, hope there are no creepy crawlies around, especially slugs, that slime all over my coat, yuck.

I tried to hide, as I always do, but Dick found me and has dropped me on the fairway.

Good stroke that one, didn't feel a thing. That's

how it is when I am hit properly maybe this guy is better than I thought.

Just a couple of yards from the green and 30 from the flag stick.

A nice wedge shot Dick!

That was good, because it slid under to lift me not hit me, which doesn't hurt as much as the other clubs do.

What I don't like is going down that deep black hole. In fact I will do all I can to stay out of it.

Spike marks, pitch marks that other thoughtless players leave on the green, bits of grit, broken sea shells and even the odd weed the greens keeper has missed. They all help to fulfil my one aim in life, to stay out of that deep dark hole.

I like the putter, which will be used next, because I don't get hit very hard.

Four feet from the hole, I'm determined not to go in for 5.

I have been putted straight towards the hole and if I move a little I can catch that spike mark and miss the hole.

Yes! Missed!

Dick is not pleased. He just called me a little asshole, not very nice.

I hope the lady golf balls don't hear such language when they go round.

I have heard of some lady balls being mistakenly put into a man human's bag, there was hell to pay.

They were in an awful state when they got back to the club house.

One was so traumatised she had turned pink with embarrassment. Poor thing, needed a double wash and polish to get over the shock.

Sorry about that but it makes me so mad.

Anyway, the inevitable is about to happened, I am being putted into the black hole.

Here I go, down into the black abyss.

It's always dark down there but the first hole always seems the worst. At least it's not full of water, because I don't like getting wet.

My one real dread is that one day I will fall into a hole without a bottom. I know it won't happen but there is always that thought because you rarely get the chance to look in before you fall in.

Thankfully that's the first hole over.

2nd HOLE

Par 4

This par four should be fun, a dog leg to the left.

This is just the type of hole a right handed human with a slice dreads.

The wood is out again so I am due for another good spanking.

Ouch, here I go again slicing straight for the trees.

Wow! I missed again.

Although it gives me a head- ache, I must try harder to hit some trees, then I can find some really deep rough.

Luckily for Dick I can see the green from where I

am sitting so it's a clear shot.

Dick is looking rather worried, no doubt because he knows he has as much chance as a snowball in hell of getting through that gap in the trees.

I don't believe this!

Dick is only going to try and use a two-iron out of here, which only goes to prove once again that these high handicappers are from the hit and hope brigade because, as any golfer worth his salts, in this position it's getting back on the fairway which is important, not distance.

Here we go, ouch, ouch, ouch.

One stroke, two trees and I'm back where I started,

I am getting more verbal abuse from Dick, as if it's my fault, which of course it is.

Dick is now going to use his five-iron, which is a much better choice.

Out onto the fairway at last, now it's to the green.

That was quite a good shot, about six feet from

the green and ten yards from that awful black hole.

Dick is going to use a putter, which could get me quite close but I can see a nice piece of shell about a yard from the hole.

Here I go, got it, nicely pushed to the side of the hole, just a short putt now.

Oh dear, I missed again and once more I am a little shit.

If looks could kill he would have me relegated to the driving range right now.

What these humans don't seem to realise is

that a ball with any balls
has to miss short putts
sometimes just to keep the
game interesting.

Just to be nasty I've
been put down that black
hole once again.

3rd HOLE

Par 3

A par 3, humans call this a short hole, heavens knows why!

They seem to take just as many shots as they do on the long holes.

The nine-iron has shot me right up in the air, it's a great view but I don't like heights, it makes me feel sick.

Yes, I may be a golf ball but I have feelings too and the sooner I get down from here the better.

It's quite windy up here so I am sure I can use this to my advantage to miss the green.

This green is elevated so if I catch the down slope to the right side I will bounce into the scrub and bushes, great move.

In I go about four feet, serves him right for making me feel sick.

Now I guess Dick is feeling sick too if the word shit he just said is anything to go by.

Temper, temper Dick.

My god there's a worm cast about an inch away from me, boy does it stink.

OK, ok, to humans it doesn't mean much but to a golf ball it's a smelly pile of shit as big as I am, so Dick, hurry up and take your next shot.

Bloody hell that hurt, so for that shot it's over the green and down the other side.

Great roll, managed to get into the rough.

That shot felt good, I finished about four feet from that black hole.

I will go straight in this time so that I can get a good clean, then that worm stink will go away.

4th HOLE

Par 4

Sitting on the fourth tee makes me wonder why I ever came out today.

Stretching before me is a great expanse of water, I hate water!

Because humans have some strange desire to hit balls into the water I know that there is a bloody good chance I will end up in there too.

Dick is about to spank me over the water onto the fairway on the other side.

What a joke, Dick has got as much chance as me ending up as a hole in one.

Told you, hit low off the tee heading straight for the water and Dick has just called me a little bastard.

As I have been hit at such a low trajectory I will be able to skip myself on the surface of the water and onto the fairway, made it, just.

Sticky mud is not exactly my favourite place to be but it's better than in the water.

The one consolation is that now Dick has seen where I am he likes it even less than me.

The next stroke should splash mud all over his nice white shoes and light blue trousers. Some humans do wear strange coloured clothes.

Bad language from Dick once again, just because I have only travelled twenty yards from the water and Dick is one muddy mess. Boy is he pissed off now.

Mind you, so am I. My lovely white coat is in one hell of a mess too.

That shot felt quite good and I am now just off the green.

This can't be right, after all the trouble on this hole Dick has just chipped me to within a foot of you know where.

I guess there is no alternative but to get this over with and get cleaned up.

5th HOLE

Par 5

This hole should be interesting, it is a par five. Most high handicap humans like long holes because for some reason if they end up with an 8 or 9 they use the excuse that it's the longest and most difficult on the course. They won't just admit that they were playing crap golf.

Once again I am on my way and once again I have been sliced and heading for the trees on the right.

Crack.

Oh boy, am I going to have a headache after that.

Dick has got the most goddamn awful slice I have ever had the misfortune to be involved with.

I am now deep in the trees but in the open. No shot forward, just out sideways back onto the fairway.

I try hard not to think about being here in the trees, alone and unloved by Dick, through no fault of my own I might add. Unseen creepy crawlies all around, with a bad headache and knowing I will only get sworn at when Dick does find me and sees the shot he hasn't got.

Two strokes later and I am back on the fairway.

This time it's a good shot, now just a wedge to the pin.

Another nice shot, my human is starting to get a little better.

Right to the heart of the green, I hope he remembers to mend his pitch mark.

A friend of mine was out last week with a human

who left nearly every pitch mark he made. He was so upset he made sure he got lost on the last hole to save the embarrassment of explaining to the other balls back in the clubhouse what his human had done.

The last we heard he had made it back to the driving range pen where he was recovering well.

I have been putted to within 2 feet of the hole, I guess I will make Dick happy on the next putt so I will go into that horrible hole, then maybe he will be nicer to me.

That's it, I'm in. Dick does look pleased with himself, I can't understand why, he took seven and I did all the work!

6th HOLE

Par 4

This hole is a blind hole, by this I mean the fairway goes up a hill and the green is down the other side out of sight.

The idea is to drive me in the vicinity of the direction flag, which is placed at the top of the hill in the middle of the fairway.

Impossible! For the first time Dick has hit me straight and I am heading towards the direction flag but I have managed to roll into a divot.

After his best drive he will not be pleased. I will

cover my ears so that I can't hear his verbal assault on me.

Humans don't realize that not all golf balls have got a thick skin.

Humans know that playing from a divot can make the ball do strange things.

Dick has decided to play a sand wedge just to get out of trouble and to keep out of more trouble.

It has added another shot to his score, which is the whole idea of me being there.

I am now heading for the
edge of the green, if I roll
just through a little I can
end up in the sand trap,
That's it, into the sand.

The last place Dick
wanted to be.

As far as I am
concerned the only
problem for me is that the
sand seems to get into
every one of my dimples.

Two strokes later and I
am still in the sand.

Dick is just about to
explode and saying fucking
traps, has relieve his
frustration for the time
being.

I guess I will jump out on Dicks next shot.

Now 10 feet from the pin, it will be so easy to miss the hole because of all the grit, pieces of shell and sand on the green, which have been shot out of the trap with the balls. I have missed and again and now in at last.

just missed double figures, the big O. I will take great delight in telling the guys back at the clubhouse about the nine I made on the sixth hole.

Anything over eight and we get a special mention at our next ball meeting.

Dick, on the other hand, has vowed to throw me in the fucking lake when he has finished the round.

7th HOLE

Par 3

On a nice day like this why oh why do I put myself through this torture?

I try to please my human by visiting all parts of the golf course so that he gets his money's worth, how does he thank me? By swearing at me all the time and hurting me most of the time when he hits me with his clubs instead of it feeling nice and smooth when I'm hit.

Humans call it timing, what a joke, with Dick, most of the time it's hit hope and humiliation.

Having said all that, this hole should be the best of the round, a par three, down hill 160 yards straight ahead.

That was another crap shot, he just topped me and I am going straight along the ground between the bunkers and up onto the green, what a fluke.

Would you believe it, Dick is now congratulating himself on a good shot. Mind you, the other humans are looking daggers at him.

This could be because they all take part in what

they call betting, which involves the giving and taking of paper at the end of the game.

At this time some humans get quite agitated and others very happy. Strange, very strange.

Dick is about to putt me from 5 yards for a birdie.

A birdie is the last thing he deserves after the last shot.

Straight at the hole but a bit fast so I will jump straight over the hole and finish that knee knocking 3 feet past the hole.

More abuse, another miss, boy is he pissed off again, time for me to hide in the hole.

8th HOLE

Par 4

This next hole has got a small dyke on the right hand side running the whole length of the fairway and halfway around the green.

The big problem with this is that Dick has this bad slice. In fact, to be honest, it's more like a half a loaf.

Hello! This is a new strategy by Dick he is taking his slice into account and addressing me about twenty degrees to the left in the hope that this will compensate for his slice.

As I have seen so many times before, this is a big mistake because I will make sure I go dead straight.

Here in the rough on the left of the fairway I have just seen Dick threaten to break his golf club in half, no doubt he is swearing too.

That is so satisfying after all the hard work I have done. Of course, the greatest reward for a golf ball is to frustrate his human so much that he actually does break his club.

Back at the clubhouse I would be greeted as a hero if this did happen. This is what we all strive for.

I have just heard a noise in the longer grass it's getting closer, phew! It's only a hedgehog, just missed me with his spikes.

You may think that I am being silly but to me the spikes are the size of javelins, would you like to be poked with a javelin?

Dick has found me and he is playing me out of this

short rough, about a seven- iron from the green.

Now is my chance to get into the dyke around the green.

That's it, one bounce on the green and over into the dyke.

Although I dislike water it is only four inches deep and to see Dicks face is worth the ducking.

Because I am unplayable Dick has dropped me away from the green on the other side of the dyke.

This is another problem for weekend golfers

because if they have to play over anything but the fairway, we balls invariably end up in whatever hazard they are playing over. Shame!

Well he surprised us all, including himself, I am on the green and even more remarkably only 2 feet from the pin.

Because of the last shot I will go straight into that horrible hole on the first putt.

There, what a nice ball I am, I just hope no other ball was watching when I did that or they will think I have gone soft and we can't have that can we?

9th HOLE

Par 4

I can see the clubhouse from this tee straight in front of me 460 yards away.

I have noticed that one of the other players has given Dick advice on how to stop a bad slice. It was to keep his head still and to stop trying to knock my coat off, sound advice indeed, what happens next should be interesting.

What a great stroke, felt good just a little slice and I have finished on the fairway.

Oh dear! Dick is about to use a fairway wood for the

first time this could be a disaster because quite good golfers find it difficult to use this club well.

This is my chance to make Dick do the dreaded and very embarrassing air shot. I will nestle down in the grass as he swings.

Dick has missed!

Now we have the furtive and embarrassed look around in the hope that other players haven't seen his miss, and if they didn't, to pretend it was a practice shot.

These humans are a real sneaky lot. Cheating comes to mind.

The smiles after the good drive have gone to be replaced with murderous looks at me and that well used word shit has been uttered once again. One thing about Dick, he does say shit with great feeling.

Ouch, that hurt a lot and no wonder, I have been topped into the ground and only moved a few yards and once again it's all my fucking fault.

A slight smile again now because of a much better shot this time.

As Dick swore at me again I am determined to make him look a real hacker by the clubhouse so here I go straight into the deep sand trap to the left of the green, not the place to be.

Two shots later, scratched and bruised, I'm on the green covered in sand, the things I do for my golf ball society. Still I'm expected to make some sacrifices.

Now clean and ready for the putt, bloody hell that was hard, mind you 30 feet is a long way.

Short by 3 feet and in for an eight and a quick exit from the green by my rather embarrassed Dick and a Dick is exactly what he is.

10th HOLE

Par 4

This is a short par 4, so Dick is going to use a long iron for position on the fairway.

What a laugh, he is kidding himself. The only thing he will do is try to hit me too hard to make up for not using a wood off the tee. I have seen it so many times before. It's all in the mind of these high handicap humans. Timing doesn't enter their heads.

I was right! Dick has topped me 50 yards down the fairway.

I now have an unhappy Dick.

Oh no! Not the fairway wood again, this could be even more embarrassing.

Ouch! I have been hit right on the top which has pushed me into the ground and then out onto the fairway again 12 feet further on, he is even more unhappy now and bollocks is the new expletive

What humans must realize is that the more they get mad the more they lose concentration and the worse their round becomes.

Here is a fine example of that, Dick is going to use a fairway wood again.
Will he never learn?

I am now in the middle of a huge slice and heading for the woods.

I have landed in a bunch of old rotting leaves about 15 feet into the trees and a sideways chip out onto the fairway is the only shot.

I can hear something moving in the leaves, shit! Sorry, this human golf talk is catching.

It's a huge slug heading my way. This is awful it's climbing all over me.

Humans might not think this is a big deal but just remember, if I was a human this slug would be the size of a car. I wonder how they would like it all over them.

The slug has gone now but left a trail of slime all over me, disgusting! Boy do I need a wash.

I'm back in play about 50 yards from the pin.

A good shot at last onto the green. I will now get that greatly needed clean, a good putt too, finished 2 feet from the pin, a putt down that horrible place

and up for a proper wash
and clean.

11th HOLE

Par 5

Another par 5 and another chance for Dick to try for double figures.

You can tell I have no great confidence in Dick's ability as a golfer.

What a great surprise, from the tee I am on the fairway again and Dick is looking very pleased with himself. I guess he has to make the most of the few good shots so far.

Would you believe it! Dick is going with a fairway wood again. I guess he is all fired up because of his tee shot. Normal situation resumed, slice mode again and heading for the trees.

This is amazing! I have managed to hit a large oak tree and I have ended up back on the fairway.

To be honest I didn't fancy being back in creepy crawly grass right now.

Dick is looking pleased again, with luck like that I guess he should. Mind you, his playing partner is looking to the heavens in disbelief.

A good five-iron should see me on the green but instead I am heading for the sand trap in front of the green.

The problem for Dick is that there is another trap just in front of this one.

High handicap humans have a real problem here because to get out of this trap and fly the other one onto the green would be a very good shot for a good golfer, it would be a miracle for Dick.

First shot, still in the same trap, second shot, now in the second trap, third shot, still in second trap, fourth shot, on the green at last.

Dick has just called me a little bastard again.

This may be true but what a thing to say to a ball with such an outstanding name. He will get a 10 for that.

Dick has putted me to within 4 feet a ringer would be good right now.
Yes! Dick has just putted me in for the big O, 10. Embarrassed, you bet.

It just goes to prove swearing at me or any other golf ball doesn't pay.

12th HOLE

Par 3

This par three is about as easy as they come.

I am sitting on the tee peg looking down on the green, which is 110 yards away. A nice easy wedge should do fine.

No such luck, Dick was so interested in where he thought I had gone that he forgot the most important rule of golf, watch the ball until you have hit the bloody thing.

He has once again topped and hurt me, I am now rolling down the hill towards the green, you guessed, also heading for yet another sand trap. I wonder how many strokes it will take to get me out this time.

Incredible, Dick has blasted me out of the sand straight into the hole.

You should see this!

Dick is dancing up and down like a man possessed. The word fuck is being used again but this time in a happy way.

It is strange that this human word fuck, can be used when they are happy, sad or really upset.

13th HOLE

Par 4

Dick looks rather subdued about this hole and little wonder because one hundred yards the fairway is cut onto the side of a hill running down from left to right.

If my human does a slice, which he normally does, I will, without doubt, end up in the trees at the bottom of the hill.

To compensate for this Dick is again aiming well to the left.

This time it has worked, I have missed the trees on the left and the slice has left me in the fairway. Unfortunately I have rolled into a seagull splatter it's disgusting and smells of fish.

One consolation about being covered like this is, when Dick hits me he could get splattered with it too. Well I can always hope.

On impact the face of the club has squirted some of the splatter onto Dick's golf glove. Now part of his pristine white glove is stained yellow with green streaks.

According to Dick, that shot just cost him, a new fucking golf glove.

I am now just on the edge of the green about 24 yards from the pin. A good putt to within 2 feet of the hole, another putt and I am down for four.

Credit where it's due, the approach and putts were good.

I have noticed a strange look in dicks eyes, my god, no, Dick has decided that I need a good clean because I am dirty and no doubt smell a bit fishy.

I am heading for the one thing balls dread above all, to be scrubbed by a bristle brush, that's right, I am going into the ball washer. to be twisted around and up and down in soapy water is bad enough but to have a stiff bristle brush scrubbing you all over at the same time is the last straw.

I will play up on the next hole big time, you see if I don't.

14th HOLE

Par 5

Now I have had my wash and brush-up and I am ready for this par 5.

As I said before, humans like par 5's because most of the time the smaller courses are short enough to reach in two shots, with a bit of luck thrown in, a bloody big bit of luck if you are playing with a guy like Dick.

It is also payback time for putting me in that ball washer.

I will start by falling off the tee peg. This really makes golfers mad, especially if you time it right at the end of their preparation just as the top of their swing. It makes them feel like a right pillock, which in turn puts them off their next stroke. I did tell you what would happen but this is different altogether, a duck hook into the long rough about seventy yards from the tee.

Although I don't like the long grass with all the creepy crawlies that go with it, I'll put up with it because it's payback time.

Dick has hacked me out onto the fairway some 35

yards further on, only 400 to go.

Oh dear! Dick is taking his two- wood out of the bag again. I don't believe this he has hit me as straight as an arrow and a long way.

Not much I could do with that shot I am now only 130 yards from the green.

No matter how good he thinks the next shot is I will make sure that I end up in the greenside rough.

To be honest, I have been in so much sand in this round my friends could start calling me sandy, so a bit of rough will make a nice change.

After that last shot I am sitting in the rough just above quite a slope leading down to the pin.

Too much club here and I can roll well past the hole.

Dick has just fluffed his shot by hitting the ground before the ball but unbelievably the movement has popped me just onto the edge of the green and I have started very slowly to roll down the slope towards the hole.

Try as I might I can't stop myself, Closer and

closer, oh smiley balls, that's golf ball swearing if you must know, I'm going straight into the hole.

This is not supposed to happen on a payback hole of all holes.

Dick is being over exuberant with his celebrations once again.

You do look a prize prick Dick, when you do that.

15th HOLE

Par 4

I wonder how Dick will stand up to the last four holes because after the last fourteen holes he is looking a bit knackered.

Now Dick has a short par four of 325 yards but with a very small elevated green, which I like a lot because I can miss it easily.

There is one large solitary sand trap about 260 yards from the tee. This trap has a very high eyebrow, this means that if I can end up short of the sand and in line with the hole my human can't see the green.

You can guess where I am, that's right, in the trap.

Dick has played what I will begrudgingly call a good blind shot which is actually heading right to the centre of the green.

A slight adjustment and I can bounce off into the second cut and nestle down nice and low. To get right over the green from the next shot should be easy.

Not a bad stroke but I will just roll off the other

side and according to Dick I am a shit head golf ball.

The first cut is short so Dick is going to use his putter.

That was a good put just 3 feet to go.

Lots of spike marks to guide me past the hole, which they have.

Dicks face is again a picture of disbelief and fuck is his word of frustration because he has missed yet another short putt.

Dick has not yet grasped the fact that putting is a skill in itself.

Unfortunately Dick has a lot to learn and if he is impatient he will never become a good golfer.

A gimmy putt and its in the hole for a six.

16th HOLE

Par 3

This par three is nice and short, 95 yards straight ahead with a flat green. If Dick doesn't par this hole he may as well find another sport to be crap at.

As I am nearly home I will be kind to Dick by making him think he is good when he gets a birdie two.

Everything is going fine, a good swing, nice and high and down onto the green about 10 feet from the pin. I said I would be kind to Dick and I am, at the moment.

He has got such a look of satisfaction on his face.

Hang on! Something new is happening to me, Dick has spat on me to get the grass mark off my coat.

After me being so nice to him he goes and does that, it's a disgusting thing to do.

You must appreciate the fact that compared to a human I am very small so a human spit is like a cup full to me, not nice.

Because of this new development in our

relationship I will now proceed to make him miss the next two putts and take great delight in listening to him swearing at everything but his own pathetic putting, serves him right.

The longer I am with Dick the more I think his name really suits him.

17th HOLE

Par 4

The seventeenth is 385 yards to the pin the big problem for Dick is to avoid the creek which runs across the fairway 130 yards from the green.

As Dick has proved so many times before, he can't use a driver.

Dick must have heard me because he is going to use a three wood.

Good thinking, I should end up short of the creek. Like hell I am! I am sure I can reach the creek if I try hard enough.

Great roll just made it over the edge and I am sitting in an inch of water.

Bloody hell the water's cold today I hope Dick lifts me out quickly.

No such luck, after the inevitable abuse aimed at me the idiot is going to play me from where I am in an inch of flowing water resting on gravel, even a professional would do well to get out of this.

You would think his friends would tell him to take a drop.

I guess they don't because they want a good laugh too.

Here comes the club head, crash, silence, then, fuck fuck fuck, all that frustration, maybe it's because I have only moved two inches and the water has splashed all over his clothes and into his face and to make things worse he has made quite a mess of his club too.

Dick has now decided he is not a professional and has dropped me on the fairway on the tee side of the creek.

After that shot I am lying just in front of one of the traps guarding the green and Dick will have to play over it to get to the pin and we all know what that means.

Because Dick thinks I don't like him he will blame me for all his bad shots including the next one and you can guess where I will end up.

Yes, Dick has played me straight into the trap or was it just me playing up again?

That was good, out first shot about 9 feet to the pin.

As the round is nearly over I guess I can be a little generous and let Dick putt me into the next to last black hole.

18th HOLE

Par 4

At last I am on the eighteenth tee.

This has been one hell of a long round of golf, in more ways than one.

Distance and time come to mind. That's apart from all the abuse I have taken in the last five hours. Well, I did say it was a long round! However, I do feel sorry for the four humans behind, they have had to wait before they could play so many times.

This final hole is only 400 yards long but with a narrow fairway lined with trees and a saucer shaped green which is surrounded by sand traps.

A good tee shot, I am on the fairway 100 yards from the green but just to make it interesting I have managed to roll into another divot. This will make it a difficult shot once again for Dick.

It might be the last hole but I still have my job to do, which as we know is to frustrate and annoy Dick. I will just cover my dimples until the air is not so blue.

If Dick doesn't calm down before he takes this

next shot I could end up anywhere. I say this because the green is positioned right in front of the clubhouse which is only ten yards from the back sand trap.

Being so close to the clubhouse it can be instant embarrassment for any human who plays a crap shot to this green. Sods law there will always be someone watching if they do.

Oh shit, I have just taken off like a bat out of hell, bounced on the back of the green over the bunker and smack, right into the big picture window of the clubhouse, off again, a bounce onto the path, over another trap and back onto the green, coming to rest only six feet from the pin.

What an adventure that shot was! It must be one of the most bizarre shots the eighteenth has ever seen.

I can hear Dick whooping with delight as if it was a great shot.

You might have guessed it would be Dick that would do that to me, I may never live this down.

Would you believe this! Dick is being cheered onto the green with high fives all round, how pathetic, I can only think they are taking the piss, I know I am!

Go on then putt me out of my misery into that black tube for a birdie.

What the hell am I thinking of, capitulation is not the name of my game.

Even though I have been sworn at, beaten, scratched, cut and bounced out I have just enough strength to make sure another birdie is not for Dick's card.

That little piece of shell from the path will be just enough to guide me past the hole.

That's it, now Dick can putt me in for his very lucky Par four.

My last indignity, Dick has just kissed me.
Yuck!

THE NINETENTH

THE BAR

This is what humans call the Clubhouse or to be more precise the BAR at the Clubhouse, but before the bar it is the locker room.

This is *not* the place to be for the faint-hearted golf ball. The sights, sounds, smells and swearing are something to behold, I just hope a lady golf ball never gets in here by mistake. It could do her lasting damage and she could end up spending the rest of her days caged up in the driving range with all the other inmates.

Horror of horrors because the driving range is normally occupied by cheap, shifty looking, striped coated rejects. They are always trying to escape over the fence but they are normally found and returned with a whack up the ass by a passing human.

Part of the locker room is the shower room, not a place I normally go but I happened to roll in there the other day and boy what a shock I had. There in front of me were all these naked steaming humans with two balls of their own. I just couldn't figure it out what they needed me for!

Now to the nineteenth hole proper, the bar.

This is where humans sink drinks not balls, get rowdy, swear and bullshit about what a great round they have just had if it hadn't been for a few bad lies, bounces and a crappy ball.

As all you humans know only too well, my friends and I are the only ones who really decide what sort of round a human is going to have.

Refreshingly, we do sometimes hear a human say:-
That's the last time I will ever play that fucking stupid game again!

With those satisfying words ringing in my dimples I will now retire to my box with a smile on my face, put on a nice clean white coat and reflect on all the frustration I have caused Dick today.

Maybe tomorrow I will be lucky and get a low handicap human, not a prick with a stick, like Dick.

Ah well, I can dream.

GUTSY